1 0/22

Magic

A Mystery
for Megan

Abi Burlingham

PICCADILLY PRESS • LONDON

For Toby and Emma,
with love

First published in Great Britain in 2012
by Piccadilly Press Ltd,
5 Castle Road, London NW1 8PR
www.piccadillypress.co.uk

A catalogue record for this book is available
from the British Library

ISBN: 978 1 84812 242 0 (paperback)

Printed and bound by CPI Group (UK) Ltd, Croydon, CR0 4YY
Cover design by Simon Davis
Cover illustration by Susan Hellard

Things Megan Didn't Know

Megan was nine, and for a nine year old there were lots of things she knew. She knew all the primary colours and her times tables up to ten. She could make the best cheese toasties in the world and she knew that if you got bored you should use your imagination; her mum was always telling her so.

She could count to twenty-nine in French and knew how to knit long scarves for Flopsy, her favourite snugly bunny, because her mum had taught her. The only thing she couldn't do was cast on and cast off, because those bits were too difficult, even for a nine year old who knew lots of things.

But there were also lots of things that Megan didn't know. She didn't know that she would be moving to Buttercup House and she didn't know that there were mice who lived there who seemed to be able to tell the time. She didn't know about the mysterious black cat and beautiful golden dog and she didn't know that the little girl, Freya, who lived next door would become her best friend . . . and she had no idea why Buttercup House was called Buttercup House.

A Normal House
in a Normal Street

Megan had always lived in a normal house in a normal street with a normal-sized garden and an average sort of garage at the side. She had no brothers, no sisters and no pets. She often wished she did.

Her mum was an artist and made interesting things out of clay and her dad worked in an office and went out in a suit in the morning and came back in the same suit at night.

Megan had a friend called Emily and a friend called Beth. She liked her house in the normal street with the normal-sized garden and the average sort of garage at the side, and she liked her friends Emily and Beth.

But sometimes Megan got bored, even though she tried very hard to use her imagination, like her mum told her. Sometimes she and Emily and Beth had played every game they knew how to play, had ridden their bikes up and down the road and had hidden in every place they could think of. Then they got fed up and went back to their own homes to sulk.

'You shouldn't sulk,' her mum said.

'But I'm bored,' said Megan.

'Then use your imagination,' said her mum.

Megan would try, and sometimes it worked. She would fill the spaces in her head with a game where she lived in a big house with a big fluffy dog called Boots, and two older brothers called Joshua and

Jack who would look after her and give her piggyback rides and lollies, especially strawberry ones. Megan loved strawberry lollies.

Then the sign went up in their front garden. It said *For Sale* in blue letters on a yellow board. A man came and knocked it in with a big wooden hammer and the noise echoed down the street.

'Where are we going?' asked Megan. She knew her dad had found a new job and that they might have to move, but it hadn't seemed very real until now. She had been far too busy playing with Emily and Beth even to think about it.

'We've found a house,' her dad said, 'with lots of space for your mum so she can make more things.'

'What about school?' Megan asked.

'There's another school,' her dad said. 'You'll love it.'

'But what about Emily and Beth?' asked Megan.

'You can write to them and they can come for a

sleepover,' her mum suggested.

But Megan didn't want to leave her friends. She didn't want to hardly ever see them and she really didn't like the thought of having no one to play with.

The Move to Buttercup House

Megan didn't see Buttercup House until the day they moved in.

'We want it to be a surprise,' her mum said.

And it was a surprise! The house was huge, and looked . . . well, tumbledown, as her grandma would have said.

As she walked through the front door, the first thing Megan saw was a wooden floor and she wondered where the carpet was. Then she noticed a small pile of fresh mouse droppings. Of course, Megan didn't know they were mouse droppings because she had never seen mouse droppings before. Megan saw small, round, brown blobs and wondered what they were. If Megan had looked a few seconds earlier, she would have seen a small brown mouse watching her very carefully.

Then Megan looked up and saw that she was in a long, narrow hallway with a big stairway climbing up the right-hand side. Megan thought that, if it wasn't for the wall holding it up, it would have definitely tumbled down. It was like an old person that needed propping up. Megan looked at her mum, and her mum smiled one of her *I know what you're thinking* smiles.

'It's not that bad, Meggy,' she said.

'Nothing a hammer and a few nails can't fix,' her dad said.

They walked through a door that was barely

hanging on by its hinges and into the kitchen. Megan stared at the door. *Tumbledown,* she thought. *Definitely tumbledown.*

'Just look at those views,' her mum called to her. 'This is what we came for.'

Megan was still staring at the door, wondering how a hammer and a few nails could fix it.

'Meggy,' her dad said. 'Come here.'

He guided her through the large square kitchen to a stable door that opened on to the back garden. It was a beautiful spring day. Megan stared out of the door. She felt her feet fix to the spot and couldn't move.

Through the doorway she saw a garden bigger than any garden she had ever seen. It stretched out before her, rolling downwards, dotted with trees whose arms reached towards the clouds. Then Megan's mouth fell open. To one side was an enormous tree, and in it was a treehouse.

'A treehouse!' Megan screamed. *Emily and Beth*

would love it, she thought. *Especially Beth. She loves dens.*

'It's great, isn't it?' said Megan's mum.

'It hasn't been used for years,' her dad added. 'We can fix it up though.'

At the bottom of the garden were more trees, then more grass that seemed to go on forever.

'Is all that ours?' Megan asked.

'There's a small stream at the bottom, just beyond those trees,' Megan's dad told her. 'Then just beyond that there's a fence. Up to the fence is ours.'

'And whose is the rest?' Megan asked, wondering who owned the field and wood beyond.

'It all belongs to the people next door,' said Megan's mum.

'Who are the people next door?' asked Megan.

'There are a mum and dad, just like us, a little girl about your age and her granny.'

Megan was beginning to feel a whole lot better about Buttercup House. The garden which went on and on forever was definitely something to feel pleased about, and the treehouse was something to feel very excited about. There was the little girl next door too. They could play hide and seek for ages in this garden, and as her dad had said, a hammer and a few nails could fix the rest.

The Rooms
in Buttercup House

Megan was used to a house with a living room and a kitchen with a table to eat at. She was used to a house with a bathroom, a bedroom for her mum and dad and a small bedroom for herself. She was used to a room that was five steps wide and six steps long; this was how Megan always measured things.

There wasn't a single room in Buttercup House that was five steps wide and six steps long. Even the hall with the tumbledown staircase was bigger than that. Then there was the kitchen, a separate dining room and a living room. Upstairs, was a bathroom, two big bedrooms and a smaller bedroom.

'Is this one mine?' Megan asked when she saw the small bedroom.

Her mum and dad looked at each other and smiled.

'That's going to be my office,' said her dad.

Megan wasn't quite sure what her dad did, but she knew it was to do with advertising and she knew it involved lots of paper and that he needed lots of places to put it.

'This will be your room,' her dad said, leading her down the landing. Tucked away between the two larger bedrooms was a narrow set of stairs that Megan hadn't noticed before.

'Up you go then,' her mum said.

Megan followed the stairs upwards until she reached a small square landing with a door.

When she opened the door, she saw an

enormous attic bedroom. Megan had always wanted an attic room. It was the most amazing room she had ever seen, and it was yellow, Megan's favourite colour.

'We painted it last week while you were at school,' her dad said. 'We wanted you to like it straight away.'

'Do you like it?' her mum asked, uncertainly.

'I love it!' Megan said, and she really did.

Later, when her bed was all made up, and her chest of drawers and wardrobe were exactly where she wanted them, Megan counted the steps across her room. Then she thought she must be wrong and counted again, but it was still the same. Thirty steps across and thirty steps long. A perfect square.

I must write and tell Emily and Beth, Megan thought. She missed Emily and Beth. It was hard leaving her friends behind, but she had promised herself that she would be brave and try not to think about it too much.

Megan gazed through the window at the garden rolling down towards the stream and the treehouse held up high in the enormous tree. *It is wonderful here, though*, Megan thought. *Even more wonderful than the house in the game I play in my head. If only there was a dog called Boots, then everything would be perfect.*

It wasn't until the next day when Megan met Freya and when Freya told her about Dorothy, the black cat, that Megan realised that Buttercup House was anything but an ordinary house.

The Girl Next Door and the Black Cat

On the right-hand side of the back garden of Buttercup House was a wall made of big old stones. Megan stretched up her arm and tried to be as tall as she could, but she still couldn't reach the top – it was much too high. Then, she noticed a small head at the top of the wall. It made her jump.

'Hello,' said the head, which was a very pretty head with dark shiny hair and a tiny nose.

'Hello,' said Megan.

'You won't be able to reach the top, you know, it's too high,' said the girl with the shiny hair and the tiny nose.

'How did you get up there then?' Megan asked, curiously.

'I have a special walkway,' said the girl. 'Are you the new girl?'

Megan nodded.

'My name's Freya,' she said.

'I'm Megan.'

'I know,' Freya said. 'I heard your mum call you earlier. Shall I come down and meet you at the other end of the wall?'

Megan hadn't thought about the other end of the wall. She had only just discovered *this* end. 'OK,' she said.

Freya's head disappeared, and Megan followed the wall until it ended. Freya was already there, peering over the wooden slatted fence which replaced the wall and ran down to the trees and the stream.

Freya was quite a lot smaller than Megan. She wore long stripy socks that stretched above her knees and a pair of long purple shorts that looked as if they were too big for her. She wore a yellow T-shirt covered in silver stars and she had hair that reached down to her elbows. Megan thought she looked like a little elf.

'Have you seen her?' Freya whispered.

'Have I seen who?' Megan asked, whispering too, although she had no idea why she was whispering.

'Dorothy.'

'Who's Dorothy?'

'The cat,' Freya answered. 'She's back! Haven't you seen her?'

'No,' Megan answered, feeling a little puzzled. 'Is she your cat?'

Freya laughed. 'No, not my cat. She's . . . well, she's our cat.'

'Our cat?' said Megan.

Freya nodded. 'Yours and mine. She lives here. Granny told me all about her. She used to live here years ago, then she went, but now she's back.'

Megan had no idea what Freya meant and was beginning to think she was a bit bonkers. Then all of a sudden, Freya exclaimed, 'There, look!'

Megan looked to where Freya pointed, to the trees that bordered the stream, and there was a black cat, dashing through the long grass.

'I told you,' said Freya. 'Granny was so pleased when I told her I'd seen her. I wish we could play in your treehouse.'

'It needs fixing,' said Megan. 'Everything here needs fixing. But we could play in it tomorrow, when Dad's fixed it.'

So that was how Megan and Freya got to be friends – just like that!

The Treehouse

Megan's dad took planks of wood up to the treehouse and hammered and banged, and hammered and banged some more. Every now and then Megan saw a dark head appear above the wall, and she would wave to Freya, and Freya would wave back. Then Megan saw the black cat, Dorothy, again. This time she was sitting at the end of the wall and seemed to be watching her. *Why is she doing that?* thought Megan.

Megan followed her mum into the workshop at the side of the house, where she was going to be making her interesting things out of clay. At the moment, though, it was full of boxes packed full of all their things.

'Mum, did you know that a black cat lives here?' Megan asked.

'Where?' asked her mum. 'Here?'

'Yes, here,' said Megan. 'Freya told me, and I saw her yesterday and again just now. She's called Dorothy.'

'Oh, she's probably wild,' said her mum.

That'll be it then, thought Megan. *I bet she just visits now and again. But what did Freya mean when she said that Dorothy used to live here years ago? It's all very puzzling.*

'I've finished,' Megan's dad called.

Megan raced towards the treehouse.

'Careful as you go,' he said, holding on to the ladder to steady it.

Megan's heart was racing. She stepped carefully up the rope ladder, which was more difficult to climb than she had thought. Eight steps up and she was there.

It was the best treehouse she had ever seen! It looked around the same size as her old bedroom, about five steps by six, Megan thought. Megan leaned back against one of the walls. She could see Freya's garden and if she looked out of the window she could see the stream at the bottom of the garden. Then she saw Dorothy again, dashing in and out of the trees.

'I've got an old rug you can have,' Megan's mum called from below. 'And a couple of cushions.'

Megan's dad appeared moments later, with the rug and cushions under his arm. 'Here,' he said, pushing the things through the doorway.

Megan laid the rug out and put the cushions next to each other, one for her and one for Freya.

She peered through the opening, waving to Freya.

'I'm coming down,' she called. 'Meet me at the end of the wall.'

Megan carefully climbed down the ladder. It swung a bit, but she was already getting used to it.

The treehouse was fantastic!

Freya, the Treehouse
and the Mice

Freya was at the end of the wall when Megan arrived.

'Is it finished? Can we play in it?' Freya asked excitedly.

'Yes, come on, quick,' said Megan, hopping from one foot to the other.

The girls ran across the garden to the treehouse. Megan was first up, then her dad steadied the ladder while Freya climbed up.

'It's OK,' Freya told him. 'The ladder's not as tricky as my special walkway.' She reached the top and gasped. 'Wow! It's amazing!'

'Do you like the rug?' Megan asked. 'Do you like the cushions?'

'Oh yes!' said Freya, her face alight with wonder. 'It's awesome, all of it's awesome.'

Then she remembered something. 'Biscuits,' Freya said, reaching into the pocket of her dungarees and pulling out four biscuits and some paper napkins. Freya shared the biscuits out as if she was dealing cards, and the girls munched away at them.

'You are so lucky having this treehouse,' said Freya. 'But then again, I've got Granny's stories, so I'm lucky too, aren't I?'

'Does your granny read you stories, then?' Megan asked, thinking Freya meant stories from a book.

'Oh no, she doesn't read them,' Freya said, shaking her head from side to side. 'They're in her head. Granny tells me stories about all sorts of things. Granny used to live at Buttercup House when she was little. That's how she first saw the mice.'

'What mice?' Megan asked, wondering how many other animals were going to suddenly appear.

Freya looked around to make sure no one else was listening, although there was no need to as there was no one else around.

'The mice who live here,' said Freya.

'What mice who live here?' Megan asked.

'Oh! You haven't seen them yet, have you?' Freya said, understanding Megan's confusion. 'I only got to see one for the first time this morning. Are you sure you haven't seen them yet?'

'No, I haven't,' said Megan. 'I'm not sure I like mice. Are there a lot of them?'

Freya laughed. 'Just a few.'

Megan was beginning to feel a bit worried and Freya must have noticed.

'Oh, it's OK,' she said. 'Granny has always said they are well behaved and really helpful, and the one I saw this morning was very friendly.'

Megan really was beginning to think Freya might be a bit bonkers.

'How can mice be helpful?' she asked, looking bemused.

'You mustn't tell anybody,' said Freya, in a whisper, 'but they help you to remember things, or let you know when something's happened, all sorts of things really. I would have forgotten the biscuits if it wasn't for the mouse reminding me earlier.'

Megan couldn't contain it any longer and started to laugh, and once she had started, she couldn't stop. Freya found herself laughing too, and before they knew it, the two of them were holding their tummies and complaining that their cheeks ached because they had laughed so much.

'You have got the craziest imagination ever,'

Megan said. 'My mum's always telling me to use my imagination, but yours is unreal.'

'But it's true,' said Freya. 'And there are other mysteries too. I'll tell you about those later, but keep looking for the mice and you'll see them.'

So Megan did just that, and she started to see things she had never seen before.

It's
Whiskers O'Clock

The next day was Monday – Megan's first day at her new school and she woke with a jump. There was something on her arm. She was about to scream when she remembered what Freya had said about the mice. Megan sat up and looked around her. She was sure she'd seen something scuttle away.

She rubbed at her arm. It still tickled. Then she saw it. Sitting on the far side of her bedroom was a little brown mouse. It was the sweetest thing

Megan had ever seen. It had round brown ears and long whiskers, shiny dark eyes and a little nose. It stood on its back legs, with its little front legs lifted up as if it was dancing.

'So it was you that woke me, little mouse,' said Megan, remembering what Freya had told her. *The mouse must have been reminding me that it's school today,* thought Megan. Perhaps Freya wasn't so bonkers after all!

Megan got out of bed carefully and slowly. She really didn't want to frighten her new little friend away.

'OK, little mouse,' she said. 'I'm up.'

And no sooner had she said it than the little mouse scuttled away. Megan felt a bit silly talking to a mouse . . . and yet somehow she had a feeling that the mouse understood. But how could a mouse understand her? It didn't make any sense.

Going down to breakfast, Megan noticed

something. The little brown blobs she had seen in the hallway had gone.

'Mum,' she said, as she was pouring milk on to her cereal. 'You know those little brown blobs in the hallway?'

'You mean the mouse droppings?' Megan's mum said.

Oh, that's what they were, thought Megan. 'Yes. Have you seen any mice?' she asked casually.

'Not yet,' her mum said. 'They're quite shy creatures. They don't tend to let themselves be seen.'

'Oh,' said Megan, thinking that the mouse she had seen didn't seem shy at all.

'I wonder if Dorothy has seen them,' Megan said to her mum.

Megan's mum looked at her daughter quizzically, smiling slightly, and Megan had the strangest feeling that her mum didn't believe there was a Dorothy!

Keep the Secret
in the Box

There were lots of things Megan was pleased about on her first day at her new school:

1) Freya was in her class

2) Her teacher was nice

3) She got to wear a new zip-up red cardi

4) She had cheese and cucumber sandwiches for lunch – her favourite!

'I'm so pleased you're in my class,' Megan said to Freya during first break.

'I know, isn't it great?' Freya said.

'And I think I believe you about the mice,' said Megan.

'Oh, have you seen them?' Freya asked.

'Just one,' admitted Megan. 'But I think it woke me up this morning.'

'One woke me too!' said Freya. 'I wonder why they've come back now, though.'

Megan was puzzled. What did she mean?

'Which one woke you up?' asked Freya.

'I don't know,' Megan replied, wondering how on earth you could tell which one was which.

'Well, what did it look like?' asked Freya.

'Little and cute and brown, with round ears, small beady eyes, long whiskers.'

'That'll be Whiskers,' said Freya, knowingly.

Megan looked puzzled. 'But don't they all look like that?' she asked.

'Probably,' said Freya. 'But I've decided they're all called Whiskers.'

The girls both burst out laughing, and when Alex, a boy in their class, ran up and asked them what they were laughing about, Freya gave Megan a look and held her finger to her mouth, just briefly, just long enough for Megan to see.

When Alex had gone, Freya whispered to Megan, 'Don't tell anyone about the mice.'

'Is it a secret?' asked Megan.

'Sort of,' said Freya. 'No one would believe us. Granny says it's best to keep these things to ourselves. She has this saying: *Keep the secret in the box.*'

So Megan and Freya made a plan. They would use the treehouse as their secret place and talk about their secrets there.

'We'll meet there later,' Freya said. 'I can tell you more about the mice and Dorothy, and there's something else I must tell you too.'

Megan couldn't wait for later to arrive!

A Very Strange Happening

When Megan walked through the front door, the first thing she noticed was a small brown mouse at the bottom of the stairs. And then the funniest thing happened . . . her mum walked straight past it and into the kitchen and didn't see a thing! *How can she not see it?* thought Megan. Then the mouse raced across the kitchen floor and disappeared out through the open back door.

'I'm going to be in the workshop for a few

minutes, Megan,' said her mum. 'I just have something to finish off.'

Megan hung up her school bag and went into the kitchen. She was hungry. She made herself a piece of toast, spread on some strawberry jam, put it on her favourite daisy plate and went upstairs to her room. Megan gazed out of the window at the treehouse, smiling to herself. She couldn't wait to meet Freya there later and hear all about Dorothy and the mice and the something else. Then, just as she thought *mice*, something happened. Megan turned to look at the bedside cupboard beside her, and on top of it sat a little brown mouse. Then the mouse did a very funny thing. It spun around in a circle three times and darted on to the floor. Megan blinked. Was this mouse for real? The mouse spun around three more times before darting to the door, then stopped and looked at Megan.

Megan didn't know what to make of it.

'What is it?' she asked the little mouse, and the mouse spun around three times again.

It's as if it wants me to follow, Megan thought. She remembered what Freya had said about the mice letting you know when something's happened.

'Has something happened?' Megan asked the mouse.

The mouse spun round three times again and Megan ran after it, down the stairs and through the kitchen. Then the mouse ran through the open back door and headed towards her mum's workshop.

As Megan entered the workshop, she saw what the mouse had been trying to tell her. Her mum was sitting on the floor, her hands around her ankle with a broken jug beside her.

'I don't know what happened,' she said, wincing slightly as she moved her ankle. 'What a clumsy thing I am.'

Megan picked up the jug and the handle, which had come right off.

'I think that needs mending,' said Megan's mum.

'I think *you* need mending too,' Megan said to her mum.

Megan put the jug on her mum's workbench and held her mum's hand as she hobbled into the house. As they went, Megan was sure that she saw a little brown mouse with very long whiskers, peeping from behind the kitchen door.

The Arrival of Later
and a Meeting
at the Treehouse

Later came, at last! Megan and Freya raced to their secret place in the treehouse and couldn't get up the ladder quickly enough. This time, as a special treat, Megan took her cuddly bunny, Flopsy, and dressed her in her best pink scarf.

'She's lovely,' Freya said when she saw her. 'And I've got some things to show you too.'

She opened her bag and pulled out two small

bottles of orange juice and a container with two chocolate buns inside.

'Ooh, yummy!' said Megan.

'Granny made them,' Freya explained. 'Granny makes the best chocolate buns ever. She used to run the baker's shop and she made all their cakes.'

'Did she?' said Megan.

Freya nodded. 'Mum runs it now, but Granny still makes lots of the cakes. Dad works on a ship, you know.'

Megan had never known anyone who worked on a ship before.

'He's a radio operator,' said Freya.

'What does one of those do?' asked Megan.

'Operates radios,' said Freya laughing, and setting Megan off. 'He's gone to Australia. He'll be back in a few weeks though.'

Megan tried to picture Australia as she munched her bun . . . Mmmmmm! It was the best chocolate bun she had ever tasted.

Then Megan told Freya about the very strange happening with the mouse, and how she was almost certain that the mouse had been telling her to go to her mum.

Freya nodded knowingly. 'Granny says that's just the kind of thing they do. Once, when she was little, her rabbit, Smoky, hurt his leg and Whiskers came and told her. Then once, she left a tap running in the bathroom and Whiskers told her about that too.'

'But how do they know?' asked Megan.

'I've no idea,' said Freya. 'I think they're magic mice with magic whiskers.'

The girls laughed.

Megan wondered whether to mention the mouse spinning around three times. She was afraid Freya might think she was silly, but her curiosity got the better of her.

'Do you know if Whiskers . . . you know . . . ever kind of . . . spun around?'

Megan was relieved to see Freya nodding frantically.

'Oh yes, the spinning,' said Freya. 'Granny says when it's something really important, then they spin around three times.'

'Really?' said Megan.

Freya nodded again. 'And sometimes, when more mice are needed, then a few Whiskerses come to help.'

'Honestly?' said Megan.

'Yes, honestly,' said Freya. 'They helped Granny loads of times when she was little.'

Freya then told Megan how, when Granny and her brother Jonathon were little, Jonathon had tried to climb the big tree in the garden and slipped.

'One of the mice came to tell Granny,' said Freya. 'But she wouldn't go so all the mice came out and spun around. Then she heard Jonathon shouting and realised that something was really wrong. They're all very helpful,' Freya said, as if she was talking about teachers or shop assistants and not about a lot of spinning, long-whiskered mice!

But Megan was puzzled by something. 'How come your granny used to live in my house when she was little and now she lives next door with you?'

'Because she grew up and married Grandpa and had Mum and Uncle David. They lived somewhere else then,' said Freya. 'When Grandpa died, Granny moved in next door and we moved in with her.'

Then Megan suddenly thought of something else. 'Why did you say earlier that you wondered why the mice had come back now, and about Dorothy coming back?' she asked.

'Well, Granny used to see the mice and Dorothy when she was little. Dorothy used to live here, years and years ago. Then the mice and Dorothy just disappeared,' replied Freya.

Megan giggled. 'But that would make Dorothy really old.'

'She is really old,' Freya said. 'Granny is seventy and she has known Dorothy since she was tiny.'

Megan's eyes widened with disbelief.

'It's true,' said Freya.

'But then Dorothy must be nearly seventy as well!' said Megan in amazement.

'Exactly,' said Freya.

Megan shook her head disbelievingly. 'She can't be *that* old,' she said. Megan didn't know a lot about cats, but she knew that they didn't live for that long.

'Oh, you should hear about Buttercup,' said Freya. 'He's really old too.'

'Who's Buttercup?' asked Megan.

'Well, remember I said there was something else I wanted to tell you? Buttercup is the something else. He's a big golden retriever dog. I've never seen him, of course,' Freya added. 'But Granny says he's lovely.'

'*He?*' said Megan. 'Buttercup doesn't sound like a boy dog's name.'

'It's because of the buttercups and Buttercup House,' said Freya. 'I don't know his real name. Granny can tell you all about him, if you like.'

Megan really wanted to know more about Buttercup, so they made a plan for Megan to go for tea and meet Granny the following afternoon.

That night in bed, Megan snuggled up to Flopsy. She wondered what Emily and Beth would make of all this. She could just imagine their faces and Emily shaking her head and saying, 'A cat who's nearly seventy? No way!' She was sure they wouldn't believe her. Then, the more she thought about meeting Freya's granny, the more excited she got, so that in the end she had to count to at least two hundred and fifty before she finally fell asleep. When she did fall asleep she dreamed only about magic mice and fluffy old cats and a dog called Buttercup!

Tea at Freya's with Granny's Home-made Shortbread

The next day at school went on forever. Megan was excited all day. Everything Freya had told her seemed very mysterious and Megan wasn't used to mystery. She had been used to a normal life in a normal house in a normal street. But none of what had happened over the last few days was anything like normal.

Megan tried really hard not to ask Freya

questions at school during lessons.

'Is Dorothy really that old?' Megan whispered at lunch, unable to contain herself any longer. 'And is Buttercup even older?'

Freya nodded. 'They are both ancient,' she whispered. Then she held her finger up to her lips and repeated her granny's words, 'Remember, keep the secret in the box.'

By the time Megan got home from school, she felt quite sick with excitement and went straight upstairs to change out of her uniform. She didn't see any mice on the way up, or in her room, and when she looked out of the window into the garden there was no sign of Dorothy. It was almost as if the mice and the cat had never existed.

It was a warm, sunny day, so Megan put on her favourite white T-shirt with flowers and sequins on the front. Freya was waiting by the fence when Megan arrived, just as they had planned.

'Come on,' said Freya excitedly, holding Megan's hand as she climbed through the gap in the fence into Freya's garden. 'You should see all the food Mum and Granny have prepared. Come on.'

The girls ran across the garden and Freya led Megan down the special walkway she'd mentioned. It was made from tree stumps which stretched alongside the wall like steps.

'Cover your eyes,' Freya said, as she led Megan into the kitchen. 'Now, open!'

Megan gasped. 'Wow!' she said.

Anyone would have thought half the class was coming for tea! There were chunks of warm bread, straight from the oven, a pot of raspberry jam, a bowl of grapes and a small dish of crinkly crisps. There were carrot sticks and cucumber sticks and sausages *on* sticks. Then, Freya's mum put one last plate on the table, a plate of Granny's home-made shortbread. It looked delicious!

Freya's mum was small, just like Freya, with short

dark hair and the same elfish look. 'Would you like to eat in the garden?' she suggested. 'It seems a shame to be inside on a day like this.'

'Ooh, yes please,' the girls said at exactly the same time, then said, 'Jinx!' and linked their little fingers.

They loaded their plates full of yummy things and sat in the sun enjoying their food. It was their first picnic of the year.

'I love picnics,' Megan said.

'Me too,' said Freya. 'And Dorothy.'

Megan stared at Freya. 'How do you know she likes picnics?' she asked.

'Granny told me,' said Freya. 'When Granny was a little girl, she was having a picnic with her doll and teddy and Dorothy came and sat next to her and wouldn't move until she'd finished the picnic. Granny was feeling lonely at the time too, so she thinks Dorothy came to keep her company.'

'But how would Dorothy know that Granny was

feeling lonely?' Megan asked.

'Granny said she could just tell that Dorothy knew how she was feeling,' Freya said, matter of factly.

Megan pulled a face at Freya, and nudged her with her elbow. 'You are funny, Freya,' said Megan, not really believing a word of what Freya had just said.

'It's true,' said Freya. 'You wait and see. You can ask Granny later.'

A Meeting
with Granny

They were just about to finish their picnic when Granny came into the garden. She was tall and willowy and not at all like Megan had imagined. She had expected her to be tiny, like Freya and her mum. She seemed floaty somehow, her shoulder-length white hair floating like a cloud around her face. She also had Freya's tiny nose and a lovely big smile.

'Have you tried my shortbread?' she asked Megan.

'Yes,' said Megan, nodding.

'And what did you think?' Granny asked.

'It's lovely and buttery,' said Megan.

'It's my special recipe,' Granny whispered. Then she did something funny. She looked around to see if anyone was listening, just like Freya had.

'There's a secret ingredient,' she said to Megan. 'Can you guess what it is?'

Megan had no idea.

'Lemon,' Granny whispered. 'But, shhh! Keep it in the box,' she said, winking at Freya.

'Granny,' Freya said quietly. 'Can we go somewhere to talk? You know, about the mice and Dorothy and Buttercup.'

'Yes, of course we can,' said Granny. 'Let's go and sit on the bench at the bottom of the garden.'

As they sat down on the bench, Granny bent her head towards them and said quietly, 'Now then, girls, what would you like to know?'

'Can you tell Megan some things about Dorothy?' asked Freya.

'What like?' asked Granny.

'Well, I don't understand how she can be so old,' said Megan.

'I know what you mean,' said Granny. 'But, as far as I can remember, she was always around.'

'But where did she come from?' asked Megan.

'I've no idea,' said Granny. 'She was just always there. I used to think she was looking after me. In fact, I named her Dorothy. I don't think she had a name until then.'

Megan pulled a funny face. She didn't mean to be rude but she just couldn't understand how a cat could be so old and she had no idea how a cat could look after a person!

'Then, when I was about fifteen, she disappeared,' said Granny. 'The mice disappeared too. But this is the really mysterious thing – they all appeared again the day you moved into Buttercup House, Megan.'

Megan stared at Granny. It didn't make any sense at all.

'I know, I don't understand it either,' said Granny, 'but they are back. Yesterday, a piece of my shortbread went missing. I'm sure it was Dorothy who took it.'

Megan laughed. 'What if it's not the same cat though?' she asked, the thought suddenly striking her that it could be a different black cat.

'Well, Freya said that she had a gold ring, like a sun, around her right eye, and a white front paw,' said Granny.

'She has,' said Freya, nodding.

'So it must be Dorothy,' said Granny, 'because she had those exact markings.'

Megan tried to understand, but she was finding it all very strange.

'Some things are hard to believe,' Granny said, 'but it doesn't mean they're not true.'

Megan thought this made sense and nodded.

'Tell her about Buttercup,' Freya said excitedly.

'Oh Buttercup!' said Granny, a big smile lighting

up her face. 'I haven't seen Buttercup for years either. In fact, he disappeared the same time as Dorothy and the mice and I haven't seen him since. Maybe he'll come back too. Whenever he used to be around, the buttercups would come up. So keep your eyes open for them.' She gave the girls a wink. 'I wouldn't tell anyone any of this though. Keep it in the box.'

'I shan't tell anyone,' Megan whispered.

'Oh, and by the way, I don't think grown-ups can see any of the animals,' said Granny.

'Really?' said Megan. 'Can't you see them?'

'Not any more,' said Granny. 'Freya has seen the mice and Dorothy since you moved in, Megan, but I haven't seen a single whisker.'

A Mysterious Cat
Called Dorothy

'Tell her the other bit, Granny,' pleaded Freya. 'Tell her about Dorothy keeping you company.'

'I would have been about seven,' Granny said to the girls. 'I was feeling upset because I'd been told off for something or other and had been sent to my room. Dorothy came to find me. She'd never been inside the house before, but she came up, found my room, and she jumped on to the bed with me. She lay right next to me until I was allowed to go downstairs again.'

'But how did she know where you were?' Megan asked, her eyes wide open.

'I don't know,' said Granny. 'She just knew. There's something quite mysterious about Dorothy. She did things like that a lot after that day.'

'Like when she sat with you at the picnic?' asked Freya.

'Yes, that's it,' said Granny. 'And sometimes she'd let me know if there were any hidden dangers, things that a child wouldn't notice. She always appeared at exactly the right moments. I didn't tell anyone though, and it's probably best that you don't either.'

'What I still don't understand,' said Megan, feeling more puzzled than ever, 'is why she's come back now, and why the mice are back too.'

'I don't know,' said Granny, 'unless . . .Oh no, that's just silly.'

'What's silly?' asked Freya.

'Well, maybe it has something to do with whether

a child is living in Buttercup House,' said Granny.

'How do you mean?' asked Megan, her eyes getting even wider.

'I'm not sure,' said Granny. 'The animals disappeared once I started growing up. Then, I left home when I met Grandpa. My mum and dad carried on living there for many years, then another couple lived there some time after, but there were no children, just a grandson who used to visit. That's who the treehouse was made for. Then the house was empty for a while before you moved in, Megan. Now you're here, Dorothy and the mice seem to have come back.'

Suddenly, Freya put her hand to her mouth. 'I've just thought of something,' said Freya. 'Do you think Dorothy might know if we're lonely too and tell us things, like when there are hidden dangers?'

'She might,' said Granny, smiling. 'I guess you'll have to wait and see.'

The girls looked at each other. Megan suddenly

felt butterflies doing backflips in her tummy.

'Talking of Dorothy,' said Granny, 'I ought to put some shortbread aside for her – she seems to have taken a fancy to it. I hope you've left some.'

'Oops!' said Freya. 'I think we might have eaten it all.'

'Don't worry,' Granny said, laughing. 'Why don't we make some more, especially for Dorothy, and we can make a batch for the shop too.'

'Ooh, yes please!' said Freya.

They walked back up to the house together, the two girls each holding one of Granny's hands, while Granny told them the best way to make shortbread, and then they spent the rest of the evening getting buttery and floury and messy.

Well, thought Megan later, as she lay in bed. *I never thought I'd end up baking shortbread for a mysterious cat!*

Megan's Story

The next day at school, Megan's teacher, Miss Roberts, asked them all to write a story.

'I want your story to have a character that's *really* interesting,' she said.

Megan thought about Dorothy and Buttercup. They were the most interesting characters she could think of. *I know,* thought Megan. *I'll make up a story about Dorothy and draw a picture too.*

Megan pulled out her special notebook with the

gold cover. She turned to the first page and drew a picture of Dorothy. She even drew the gold ring around her eye and her little white front paw that Granny and Freya had talked about. Then she wrote her story.

The Story of the Mysterious Cat

There once was a cat who was very mysterious. She was the oldest cat who had ever lived, and she had a gold ring around one eye and a white paw. She was as black as soot and was very big and fluffy. She loved to chase after butterflies and bounce on her front paws. Sometimes she got special treats of shortbread, and then she purred and had to brush the sugar off her whiskers.

Miss Roberts had said they should use some describing words. Megan was especially pleased with *black as soot*.

* * *

'What did you write about?' Megan asked Freya at lunchtime.

'I made up a creature called a Pungle,' said Freya.

Megan laughed. 'A Pungle!' she squealed. 'That's the funniest name I ever heard.'

'It's a Pungle with a very long nose,' said Freya, laughing too. 'And very long toes so it has to wear sandals all the time.'

'What did you write about?' Freya asked Megan, once they'd stopped laughing.

Megan looked around before she spoke, then realised that she was getting to be just like Freya and Granny!

'I wrote about a mysterious cat,' she said, nudging Freya under the table.

'Oh, how imaginative,' said Freya, laughing.

'Well, not everyone can invent a big-nosed big-toed Pungle, can they?' said Megan.

'I suppose not,' said Freya.

'Anyway,' said Megan. 'This cat bounces.'

'Why?' asked Freya, curiously.

'I have no idea,' said Megan, bursting out laughing again.

A
Big Surprise

Megan and Freya both had spellings to do for homework and they both moaned and groaned about it. Then Megan had an idea.

'Let's do them in the treehouse,' she suggested. 'We can help each other out.'

'That's a great idea,' said Freya, who wasn't too keen on spellings. So they arranged to meet later by the fence.

* * *

When Megan got home, she changed out of her uniform into her jeans, had macaroni cheese – her favourite – for dinner, then she grabbed her spelling book and went to meet Freya at the end of the fence. Freya arrived just as Megan did and squeezed through the gap in the fence.

'Dorothy's down there, look,' Freya said excitedly, spotting Dorothy near the stream.

'I wonder if we'll see Buttercup too,' said Megan. 'I wish Dorothy would come closer so I could see her properly. I want to see the gold ring around her eye.'

The girls went to the treehouse and worked really hard on their spellings. Megan tested Freya, and Freya tested Megan. Freya kept getting *Europe* wrong and forgetting the second *e*.

'Just remember it's got a rope on the end,' said Megan. 'Like our treehouse.'

'Oh yes!' said Freya, and the next time she got it right.

Suddenly, Freya looked up. She was staring out

of the window towards the trees.

'Megan. It's him,' she said, in a voice that was barely above a whisper.

Megan followed Freya's eyes. Out beyond the trees she saw the most beautiful golden dog.

'Oh my goodness!' said Megan. 'Is that really him? Is that really Buttercup?'

'It must be,' said Freya. Then she looked at Megan. 'What if Granny's right? What if he's come back because you're living at Buttercup House?'

Megan stared at Freya. She just couldn't believe that the animals coming back had anything to do with her.

The girls both watched Buttercup as he watched them through the trees. Somehow, having him there made them both feel incredibly happy, as if he was looking after them. Then he turned and padded away.

'The buttercups,' Freya said suddenly. 'There should be buttercups.'

The girls peeped through the door, and all around the bottom of the tree were lots and lots of bright yellow buttercups! It was just like Granny had told them.

Then the
Strangest Thing
Happened

The girls stood under the treehouse and stared at the buttercups, trying to make sense of everything that was happening. A movement at the bottom of the garden caught Freya's eye.

'Look, it's Dorothy,' she exclaimed, as the black cat appeared from behind a tree.

Megan couldn't contain her excitement a moment longer. She ran down the garden towards

Dorothy, and just before she reached the line of trees, Dorothy turned and ran towards her, stopping by her legs. It was the first time Megan had seen Dorothy close up and she thought she was the most beautiful cat she had ever seen. Straight away she noticed the white paw and the gold ring around her eye, just like Granny and Freya had said. Then something incredible happened.

Megan stood very still, watching Dorothy, who was looking up intently at her. Then Megan looked towards the stream, then at Freya.

'What is it?' said Freya, who had caught up with them.

'I think some of the bridge over the stream needs mending,' said Megan.

'Where?' said Freya.

'Over there, I think,' said Megan. 'Dorothy told me, kind of.'

Even as she said it, she knew how strange it sounded. How could a cat tell her anything?

The girls walked carefully towards the stream. Dorothy went ahead a little and then suddenly stopped and looked back at them.

'Look,' said Freya. 'You're right, Megan, the wood has come away a bit. It's a good job Dorothy warned us.'

The girls looked at each other in amazement.

'Did that really just happen?' asked Megan.

Freya smiled and nodded. 'Granny did say that Dorothy seemed to know things and warned her about hidden dangers, didn't she?'

'And now she's warning us too,' said Megan.

'I bet Granny's right about the other thing as well,' said Freya. 'I bet they've come back because you've come to Buttercup House, Megan!'

Megan didn't know what to say. She suddenly felt incredibly special.

'I can't believe what's happening,' said Megan, as the girls walked back up the garden. 'And I especially can't believe we saw Buttercup!'

'I can't either,' said Freya. 'I never thought I'd actually get to see him.'

But Megan still didn't understand how the fact that she was living at Buttercup House had made the animals come back. It was very mysterious and no matter how much Megan thought about it, she just couldn't make sense of it.

A Very Puzzled Megan

The next day, Megan could still hardly believe any of it. She thought about her old friends, Emily and Beth, and how she'd love to tell them all about it. Emily adored dogs and had always wanted one. She would love Buttercup. Of course, there was no way she could tell them – she'd promised to keep it a secret – but she wished she could!

'I told Granny about seeing Buttercup and the buttercups coming out,' Freya said, when they met in their secret place that evening.

'Did you tell her about Dorothy warning us too?' Megan asked. She couldn't wait to hear what Granny thought of it all.

'Yes. She was really excited,' whispered Freya. 'Granny thinks that because Dorothy told you, she's probably trying to look after you, like she used to look after her.'

This house and everything around it are full of mystery, thought Megan. She still didn't understand how Dorothy and Buttercup could be so old, and she felt she would never understand how she had been able to read Dorothy's thoughts. That made no sense at all. And why had they felt so safe and happy when Buttercup appeared?

Megan puzzled over it all evening, and at bedtime she just couldn't go to sleep. In the end, she sat up in bed, got out her special gold-covered notebook and wrote a poem about it all.

There once was a cat who came to me
and spoke to me in my head.
I couldn't stop thinking about it
and lay awake in bed.
And when we were playing
and the buttercups came up,
we felt so safe and happy
because of Buttercup.

Megan felt a bit better after writing her poem, even though she knew she couldn't show it to anyone – not to Emily or Beth, not to Miss Roberts, not even to her mum and dad. But at least she could show Freya. She could share anything with Freya.

The Buttercups

When Megan woke up the next morning and pulled back the curtains, she couldn't believe what she saw. The whole garden was alight with golden buttercups. They weren't just under the tree, they were everywhere! *Buttercup must be here*, thought Megan. *How wonderful!*

Then she remembered it was Saturday. She and Freya could play among the buttercups. They could make buttercup chains instead of daisy chains. She could make Freya one, and one for her mum. They could even make one for Dorothy and one for Buttercup.

Megan leaped out of bed, pulled on her shorts and a red and white striped T-shirt and raced down the stairs and into the garden of golden buttercups!

Freya was peering over the wall. 'Wow!' she squealed, her eyes lighting up as she saw the buttercups. 'You know what this means, don't you?'

Freya's head disappeared and the next moment she was running towards Megan, looking at the buttercups with a beaming smile on her face.

'I've never seen so many,' said Freya. 'Buttercup must be here. Come on.' She grabbed Megan's hand and the girls raced through the never-ending sea of buttercups, towards the trees at the bottom of the garden in search of the golden dog.

They were careful not to go over the bridge, so stood a couple of metres away from it, looking out across the stream and towards the wood. Then, suddenly, Freya gasped. 'Look, it's Buttercup!' she said.

Buttercup stepped out of the wood, his coat shining and glimmering in the sunlight.

'Oh, how wonderful!' said Megan, squeezing Freya's hand and feeling remarkably calm all of a sudden. She felt so happy again, just like the last time they had seen him.

Then, as they watched, Buttercup turned and disappeared among the trees.

'Oh! I wonder where he's gone,' said Megan, feeling disappointed. She was searching for him when, out of nowhere, Dorothy appeared. She sat right next to Megan, leaning against her legs. *How lovely*, Megan thought. It was almost as if Dorothy knew she was disappointed and needed comforting.

Dorothy looked up at Megan, and then at Freya.

'I have a feeling we'll see Buttercup again,' said Freya. 'I think that's what Dorothy's trying to tell us.'

'How does she do it?' asked Megan.

'I don't know. It's amazing, isn't it?' said Freya. 'Granny said that it all happened in her head. She said it was as if she could hear Dorothy's thoughts.'

'That's just how it feels to me,' said Megan.

'Me too,' said Freya.

It seemed that Dorothy and the mice were there to look after them. But what about Buttercup? Why had he come back?

Some Extra Things
for the Treehouse

Megan was dying to know more about the beautiful golden dog. Where did he come from and why had he been away so long? And now that he was back, what had it got to do with her living at Buttercup House? There were so many mysteries!

But Megan still hadn't had breakfast, and all the excitement of the early morning had made her even hungrier. She also wanted to take some more things to the treehouse. Megan had been saving up things that she thought might be useful, and some less useful things too.

She quickly ate her cereal and raced upstairs, pulling the box of things out from under her bed. She took them out one by one – a snugly pink blanket, in case it got cold; a book, in case she got bored, although that seemed very unlikely; a poster of a white horse to put on the wall; a roll of sticky tape and a pair of scissors, so they could stick the poster on the wall; a plastic container with some lollies in, in case they got hungry; and a colouring book and some felt pens.

Then she added some rolled-up bits of different coloured wool and some beads. Megan wanted to make Freya a friendship bracelet.

Megan carried the box to the kitchen. She took a few biscuits out of the tin and put them in with the strawberry lollies. Then, as she got to the door, she looked across the garden to the treehouse. *How silly of me*, Megan thought. *How am I going to get up the ladder with this lot?*

'Dad,' she said, peering into the living room. 'Can you help me carry some things to the treehouse?'

'What things?' her dad asked, peering over the top of his reading glasses.

'Just a blanket and a book and a poster and some tape and some lollies and biscuits and a colouring book and some pens and beads and things,' said Megan.

Her father laughed, and said, 'I think you might need a crane for that lot.'

But somehow they managed without a crane, and in no time at all, Megan had all her new things in her lovely treehouse.

Freya suddenly appeared at the fence and climbed through into Megan's garden.

'I've got some new things for us,' Megan told Freya excitedly.

The girls couldn't get up the ladder fast enough!

The Story of Buttercup

Megan showed Freya all the new things, laying them out on the rug. Freya loved the poster of the white horse. They stuck it to the wall and turned the box upside down to use as a table. Megan put the book, the colouring book and the pens on top of it. Then they measured the treehouse in steps. It was six steps long and five steps across – exactly as Megan had thought. The girls snuggled under the blanket, even though it was warm, and took out the biscuits. Then Freya spotted the bits of wool and the round tin of beads.

'What are these for?' she asked.

'Well . . . um . . . I want to make you a friendship bracelet,' Megan said, nervously.

'Oh, Megan!' said Freya, giving her new friend a big hug. 'Can I make you one too?'

Megan nodded, smiling from ear to ear. She really was glad they'd moved to Buttercup House, even though she did still miss Emily and Beth. *They would love it here*, thought Megan, and she promised herself she would write to them soon.

The girls chose their favourite colours. Freya chose green and purple, and Megan chose yellow and blue. They plaited the wool into bracelets, adding on the brightly coloured beads.

'Can you believe we saw Buttercup again?' said Freya.

Megan munched into her biscuit. 'I know. He must live somewhere near here,' said Megan. 'I wonder how many times your granny saw him, when he used to come.'

'She can tell you if you like,' said Freya. 'Shall we go and ask her?'

'Ooh, yes,' said Megan.

So the girls left their new things in the treehouse and went in search of Granny.

'Granny,' said Freya, bursting into the living room. Granny sat with her legs curled up on the chair, her head buried in a book. 'Can we talk to you?' Freya whispered.

'I thought you might want to,' Granny said, jumping up from her chair. 'A walk around the garden, I think.'

When they were halfway down the garden, Freya whispered, 'Granny, we've seen Buttercup again.'

'I knew it,' Granny said. 'I knew the minute I saw all those buttercups that he'd been here. How exciting!'

'Shall we show you where we saw him, Granny?' asked Freya.

'Ooh, yes please,' said Granny.

So Megan and Freya took Granny to the spot near the stream.

'He was over there,' Freya told her granny. 'At the edge of the wood, wasn't he, Meggy?'

Megan nodded. But when she looked at the trees now there was no sign of Buttercup, and she wondered if he really had been there, or if it had just been the golden sunlight shining through the branches of the trees.

The three of them stood, watching.

'Granny, can you tell Megan about when Buttercup came before?' asked Freya, suddenly remembering the reason for wanting to talk to her.

'Well, there's rather a lot to tell,' Granny said, leading the girls to the bench and sitting down with one either side of her. 'This is becoming a good place for storytelling, isn't it?' She laughed, reaching an arm around each of the girls.

Then Granny told her story.

'The first time Buttercup came was to help my brother, Jonathon,' said Granny.

'Is that the same brother who tried to climb the tree?' asked Megan, remembering the story Freya had told her.

'Yes,' said Granny. 'Only this time, he'd gone to the stream to look for newts and decided to explore. He went towards the woods and managed to fall into a ditch. He wasn't badly hurt but on his way down, he managed to twist his knee. He couldn't get out. Then it started to get dark, so my father went to look for him. But he couldn't find him so he ran to the local police station and there was a big search for him. They were out with torches looking, but they couldn't find him anywhere.'

'Didn't he call for help?' asked Megan.

'He said he did,' said Granny. 'Everyone must have been looking elsewhere when he called because they just didn't hear him.'

'What happened?' said Megan, starting to feel worried.

'That's when Dorothy and Buttercup came to help,' said Granny.

She then explained how her parents had left her at home, in the care of a nanny, while they searched for Jonathon.

'I couldn't sleep,' said Granny. 'So I sneaked out of bed and went downstairs, and there was Dorothy.'

'What did she do?' asked Megan.

'She stood right next to me and looked at me. I just knew that she wanted me to go with her, so I followed her into the garden, across the stream and into our field beyond,' said Granny. 'That's when I saw Buttercup. He was waiting on the other side of the stream. He came right up to me and looked at me in exactly the same way

Dorothy did. I knew that he had found Jonathon and wanted me to go with him.'

The girls were open-mouthed now, unable to speak. Even Freya, who had heard this story before, felt as if she'd been struck dumb.

'What happened then?' asked Megan.

'Well, Buttercup led me to Jonathon, then I went to fetch help. If it hadn't been for Dorothy and Buttercup, I don't know how long Jonathon would have been stuck there,' said Granny.

'What happened to Buttercup?' asked Megan.

'He sat with Jonathon for a while, but by the time we all went to help him, Buttercup had gone. Jonathon was convinced he'd dreamed the whole thing.'

'But what did you tell the nanny?' asked Megan.

'I said I'd heard Jonathon shouting for help,' Granny laughed. 'If I'd told her he'd been helped by a big golden dog that then disappeared, do you think she'd have believed me?'

The girls shook their heads.

'As I always say,' said Granny, 'some things need to be kept in the box.'

The girls nodded. They understood how silly the story would have sounded to a grown-up!

'Jonathon wasn't quite so adventurous after that,' said Granny. 'I saw Buttercup a few more times, but it was so long ago that I've sometimes wondered if I imagined the whole thing.'

'Oh, please tell Megan about the other times,' said Freya.

'Another day,' said Granny, keeping her voice to a whisper. 'But I will just tell you this. Buttercup helped me a couple of times, and I could always tell what he was thinking.'

'Really?' Megan said.

Granny nodded. 'Maybe, now you're here, Megan, he'll let you know what he's thinking too.'

Megan really hoped so, and crossed her fingers very tightly.

The Book of
Strange Tales

At school on Monday, Freya and Megan got a big surprise.

'We're going to the library,' Miss Roberts said, as the children chattered with excitement. 'You'll be able to join, if you haven't already, and you can borrow a book if you like.'

'Megan,' Freya said, 'we could borrow a book each and do swapsies.'

'Oh yes!' said Megan.

What with the move to Buttercup House, it had been a while since Megan had visited a library and she hadn't been to the one in the village yet.

It was a good twenty-minute walk from their school to the library and all the children were partnered up. Megan was with Freya, of course. They both wore the friendship bracelets they had made together.

'I'm never taking mine off,' Freya said.

'Me neither,' said Megan.

Megan was amazed when she saw the library. It was nothing like the one she'd been to in the city she used to live in. That one was all straight lines and glass. This library was perfectly round with two layers, like a wedding cake, and it sat on a big roundabout in the middle of a crossroads. It was made out of red bricks and had long thin windows. Megan had never seen such an unusual building.

'They call it the Victoria Sponge,' said Freya. 'Because it's like a big, round sponge cake!'

'Wow!' said Megan, once they were inside. The building looked even bigger from the inside and, if she looked straight up, she could see right up to the roof. The second floor went around the edges in a circle, like a big wide balcony.

'I'd like an animal book,' said Freya. 'Not a story book but a factual one, all about different animals.'

But there were two floors full of books and shelves and they didn't know where to start looking.

'We could ask that lady,' suggested Megan, pointing to a tall lady behind a desk. So they went up to the lady at her desk.

'We're looking for a book, but we don't know where to look,' Freya said to the lady, suddenly realising how silly this sounded.

'What sort of book?' the lady asked.

'Sort of factual,' said Freya.

'Sort of about animals,' Megan added.

The tall lady raised her eyebrows at them. 'Do you have a title?' she asked, thinking what a long day it was going to be.

'No,' whispered Freya, wondering why she was whispering.

But the lady hadn't heard her. 'Pardon?' she said.

'No!' Freya shouted, at the same time as Megan, so that it sounded really loud and everyone looked around. The girls tried especially hard not to start laughing!

The tall lady pointed to the next floor. 'Factual books are up there,' she said, looking a little bit annoyed.

'Thank you,' the girls said, and quickly retreated up the wooden staircase to the next floor.

'You do realise you're in the top layer of the cake now, don't you?' said Freya, trying not to laugh.

'That must mean I'm walking on the jammy bit,' whispered Megan, smiling and pretending her feet were sticking to the blue carpet.

'Blue jam!' said Freya, a little too loudly, so that *both* girls had to stifle their giggles.

The factual books took up a whole bookcase against the far wall. They didn't know where to start.

'I'll start down here,' said Freya. 'You look up there.'

Megan stood on a small stool and searched the higher shelves, while Freya searched the lower ones. There certainly were lots of books, but Megan couldn't see any animal ones. Then she saw something.

'Look at this,' she said to Freya, pulling out a thick book.

'What is it?' asked Freya. 'It looks really old.'

It did look very old. Its burgundy cover was crumpled and worn, and the gold writing on the front had started to fade.

'*The Book of Strange Tales*,' said Freya. 'What's that?'

'I have no idea,' said Megan. 'Shall we have a look?'

The girls sat down at a small table to look through the book. It was full of tales, all beautifully written, with little illustrations on every page.

'Let's borrow it,' Megan said. 'Then we can read it in secret at the treehouse.'

'Brilliant idea,' said Freya.

The girls spent a few more minutes looking for an animal book for Freya, and found one that was exactly what she'd wanted, then Megan joined the library. She got a brand new library card, and took out her first library book from the Victoria Sponge Library – *The Book of Strange Tales*!

The Tale of Buttercup

When the girls got home, they had to change out of their school uniforms, wash their hands, have their dinner and do their homework.

Of course, they didn't want to do any of these things, apart from the eating bit. They just wanted to read their books.

Megan put her finished homework in her bag and zipped up her cardigan. She wasn't sure why but she didn't want anyone else to know about the book, so she tucked it underneath her cardigan and ran into the garden.

'Just going to the treehouse with Freya,' she called.

'Be back by seven o'clock,' Megan's dad called after her.

Megan raced to meet Freya at the end of the wall.

'Have you got the book?' Freya asked.

Megan lifted up her cardi to reveal the book, all snuggled up underneath.

'I've got mine too,' said Freya.

They skipped eagerly through the buttercups, which were still glowing brightly, and across the garden to the treehouse.

Megan pulled out *The Book of Strange Tales*, putting it on the rug between them. It suddenly seemed like some very precious thing that they dare not touch. At last, Megan opened the old crumpled cover, and inside, on the front page, was a list of titles – the names of different tales. Then, Megan saw it.

'Freya, look!' she said.

'What is it?' asked Freya.

Then Freya saw it too:

The Tale of Buttercup   p.14

The girls looked at each other in amazement, then eagerly turned the pages until they reached page fourteen. And this is what it said:

The Tale of Buttercup

Gretton is a quiet village in the south of England and is typical of many villages. However, what makes Gretton different is that there have been stories of sightings in the village of a beautiful golden dog and a large black cat. What is particularly strange is that the same animals have been seen over many years.

The first sighting of them was in the late nineteenth century, around 1886, when a farmer's son walking his dog spotted the animals together near the woods.

No one knows why the animals appear or where they come from. The only thing that is known for certain is that the sightings are always reported by children, and that when buttercups appear, the big golden dog also appears. Thus he has earned himself the name 'Buttercup', and the big old house close to where the animals have been sighted has come to be known as Buttercup House.

'That's my house!' squealed Megan.

'And the buttercups are here, just like it says,' said Freya excitedly. 'We have to show Granny.'

The girls raced over to Freya's house and found Granny in the kitchen.

'Granny, you're not going to believe this,' said

Freya in a whisper. 'We found this book in the library and there's a story in it about Buttercup.'

'Really?' said Granny, quickly drying her hands.

They all sat around the table and the girls showed Granny *The Tale of Buttercup*.

'You see, it *is* something to do with children,' said Granny. 'I think the animals come to help children and to look after them. And look, if Dorothy and Buttercup were first seen in 1886, they are both much older than we thought.'

Freya, Megan and Granny all looked at each other in silence. They were all thinking the same thing. How on earth could an animal live to be well over one hundred years old?

An Email to Emily and Beth

The rest of the week was sunny and got warmer and warmer. Megan's mum said it was the warmest spring she could remember and even bought Megan a new sun hat. It was her favourite colour – yellow – with a big purple butterfly on the front. She loved it!

Megan kept looking out for Buttercup, but she couldn't see him anywhere. And yet the garden was still covered in buttercups. *He must be around somewhere,* thought Megan. She looked out of her bedroom window every morning, but all she saw were the trees against a big blue sky and small fluffy clouds drifting across the wide open space.

Megan tried to think of something to do to keep herself busy. Then she remembered Emily and Beth. She still hadn't written to them. She had meant to, but one thing had happened after another, and then she didn't know how to say what she wanted to say. But now she started to miss them all over again. *I know,* thought Megan, *I'll send them an email and I'll do it right now!*

She rushed into her dad's office – it was empty, just as she had hoped. She turned on the computer and opened up a new email.

Dear Emily and Beth,

I hope you are OK. What's been happening at school? Have you done describing words yet?

Then Megan thought about the story she had written about Dorothy. She really wanted to tell Emily and Beth.

I wrote a story at school about a mysterious black cat who ate shortbread. I used lots of describing words and my teacher really liked it.

She wanted to tell them that Dorothy was a real cat who had come back because she had moved into Buttercup House – how exciting was that? But they would never believe her. Then she thought about Whiskers, those lovely brown mice . . . but she couldn't tell Emily and Beth about them either. As for Buttercup . . . well, they would think she was completely crazy if she told them about the big golden dog.

Megan realised then how amazing her new life was, and how the only person she could really share it all with was Freya, her special new friend! But she really wanted to tell Emily and Beth some things, so Megan wrote:

The house has mice and needs a bit of fixing. But there is a massive garden and a treehouse, which Dad has already mended. I have put up a poster of a white horse in there and I have made friends with a girl called Freya who lives next door.

I do miss you both and I miss our games of hide and seek and how we always used to hide behind Mr Biggins's bins! Do you remember?

Please write back.

Love Megan xx

And she put a little picture of a dog at the bottom, with *WOOF* in a bubble. Megan smiled to herself. She was pleased that she had got round to writing at last, even if some things had to be kept in the box, just as Granny said.

She hoped they'd write back soon.

A Whole Day at
Megan's House

Megan and Freya were so glad when Saturday came. They couldn't wait to talk about Buttercup at the treehouse. But before they could reach the treehouse, the sky turned grey and rain started to come down in huge drops.

'Ooh, we're going to get soaked,' said Freya.

'Quick! Let's get in the house,' squealed Megan.

The girls ran through the rain and into Buttercup House. They were so glad to be in the warm and dry.

'Shall we play in my room?' said Megan. 'We could do some colouring and talk about Buttercup.'

So for most of the morning they did just that! Megan had a big floor colouring that she hadn't yet started. It was a picture of a woodland scene, with trees, birds, an owl and squirrels.

'This picture's all wrong,' said Freya.

'Why?' said Megan, puzzled.

'They've forgotten to put Buttercup in,' replied Freya.

The girls laughed.

'We'll just have to imagine him in the picture, then,' said Megan.

Freya kept touching her friendship bracelet and smiling. It reminded her of how much she loved sharing things with Megan.

At lunch, Megan's mum brought them sandwiches and crackers and grapes. Megan laid her quilt on the floor and they had an indoor picnic.

'It's a bedroom picnic,' said Megan. 'It's called a bedroomnic.'

'I've never heard of one of those before,' said Freya, laughing.

'That's because I just invented it,' said Megan.

Then they did a big round animal jigsaw on the floor and talked about Buttercup.

'I can't believe he's so old,' said Megan.

'I know,' said Freya. 'I wish we could see him properly. He looks so beautiful, but I bet he's even more beautiful close up.'

'I bet he is, and I bet his fur's really soft,' said Megan. 'I wish we knew more about him.'

'I do too,' said Freya.

'I know what we could do!' said Megan. 'Let's write a list of all the things we'd like to know about him.'

So the girls did some serious thinking and wrote a list of all the things they would like to know. They took it in turns, so that in the end the list looked kind of stripy – stripes of Megan's handwriting and stripes of Freya's!

1) How does Buttercup know Dorothy?
2) Does he come to help children?
3) How many times has he come back?
4) Where does he live?
5) Does he know the mice?
6) Has he ever tasted Granny's shortbread?
7) How old is he?

By the time they had finished writing their list, it was late afternoon and their tummies were very rumbly, especially after writing the bit about Granny's shortbread. Before Freya went home for dinner, they arranged to meet later on in the evening. They could go to their secret place and talk some more about the mice, Dorothy and Buttercup.

A Reply
from Emily

After Freya had gone, Megan popped into her dad's office and turned on the computer. There was a reply from Emily! Megan was so pleased. It said:

Dear Megan,

HIYA! Your treehouse sounds coooooool! Not so sure about the mice though!!!

Yes, we're doing **very interesting** and **exciting** describing words at school – can't you tell? I'm glad you made a new friend. Me and Beth were worried that you would be lonely.

We miss you too. Hide and seek isn't as good any more. Yes, we remember Mr Biggins's bins. How could we forget? Pooey! What a pong!

Email again soon.

Emily xx

Megan read the email over and over again. *I must ask Dad if I can print it,* she thought, *then I can keep it in the special box I have for special things.*

Megan went downstairs for her dinner. Her mum had cooked crispy jacket potatoes with cheese and beans. They were delicious! When she had finished, Megan asked her dad if he could print off the email from Emily.

'I want to keep it in my special box,' she told him.

While he was printing it for her, Megan did a bit more colouring in her room – there were still lots of white spaces which she and Freya hadn't filled in and Megan completely forgot about meeting Freya.

Suddenly, Megan felt a tickling sensation on her arm. She reached across and her fingers landed on a long tail! She very nearly screamed . . . but it was only Whiskers, and who would be afraid of a sweet little mouse?

'What is it?' Megan asked the mouse, but before it had time to show her, she suddenly remembered. She was supposed to be meeting Freya!

Megan quickly put the top on her pen and raced downstairs, with Whiskers running ahead of her.

Something
Unexpected

When Megan reached the kitchen, Whiskers had already disappeared. Megan wondered what the mice did when they weren't reminding her and Freya where to be. She imagined them in their little mouse houses, sitting around a small table playing cards . . . well, her mum was always telling her to use her imagination!

It had stopped raining, so Megan ran into the garden. The grass was still covered in beautiful, golden buttercups. As she reached the end of the wall, Freya arrived at exactly the same time. They both jumped and let out a scream.

'Oh, Megan,' laughed Freya. 'You frightened the life out of me.'

'You frightened the life out of *me*,' laughed Megan.

'Shall we go to the treehouse for a bit?' Freya suggested. 'Then we can come back here. Mum and Granny are trying out a new flapjack recipe.'

'Ooh, yum,' said Megan, licking her lips.

Suddenly, Freya gasped. She was looking down at her wrist. 'It's gone,' Freya said.

'What's gone?' asked Megan.

'My friendship bracelet,' said Freya, her eyes filling with tears.

'You had it on this afternoon. I remember seeing it,' said Megan, trying to cheer her friend up.

'I went for a walk with Granny after dinner,' said Freya, 'but I'm sure I had it on then.'

'Don't worry,' said Megan. 'Let's look for it now.'

The girls held hands tightly, keeping their eyes to the ground as they searched Freya's garden for her lost bracelet. But they couldn't find it anywhere. They reached the stream and the little bridge, but still there was no sign of the bracelet.

'Oh, where is it?' said Freya. 'I just know it's lost. I just know it.'

'Don't worry, Freya, we'll find it,' said Megan, trying her best to reassure her friend. 'Just try to remember where you walked with Granny.'

'Well, we followed the stream, then went to the wood,' said Freya.

'Then let's do that,' suggested Megan. 'Come on.'

'But it looks quite dark,' said Freya. 'It looks like it might rain again.'

'It'll be OK,' said Megan. 'We'll be quick. Come on.'

So the girls crossed the little bridge – which Megan's dad had mended – and followed the path of the stream through the field, searching all the time for the bracelet. But they couldn't see it. Every now and again, the girls looked up and noticed the sky getting darker and darker.

'Trust me to choose green and purple,' moaned Freya. 'It's not going to be easy to find in this grass, is it?'

'Don't worry, I'm sure it's here somewhere,' said Megan. She really hoped it was.

When they got to the edge of the wood, they weren't sure where to go.

'Where did you go with Granny from here, Freya?' Megan asked.

'Just over there a bit, I think,' said Freya. 'Granny saw a flower she liked, so we went to have a closer look.'

'Come on, then,' said Megan. 'It'll be OK.' She squeezed Freya's hand tightly to reassure her.

The girls walked into the wood and followed a narrow path for a while.

'Can you see the flower?' Megan asked.

'No, I can't,' said Freya. 'It was blue, like a star. I think maybe it was over there,' she said, pointing to an area of dense woodland.

The girls left the path and walked amongst the trees, trying to keep their eyes open for both the flower and Freya's lost bracelet.

'Oh, that might be it,' Freya said, spotting a small blue flower.

The girls headed towards it, all the time searching the ground too. But when they reached the flower, Freya wasn't sure.

'I don't know if it's the same one,' she said. And then she started to cry. 'Oh, I know my bracelet's gone,' she sobbed. 'And you made it for me and it was my favourite thing in the world.'

'Please don't cry,' said Megan, starting to feel as if she might cry too. 'I can always make you another one.' But they both knew that it wouldn't be the same.

'Let's just look a bit more.'

The girls walked further into the wood as they spotted more blue flowers here and there. After a while, one tree began to look just like another, and as the sky got darker and darker, it became harder and harder to see. No matter how much they looked, they couldn't see the bracelet anywhere.

Suddenly, Megan stopped. 'Freya, where are we?' she asked.

The girls both looked. All around them were trees. There was no sign of the fence or the stream. And it was dark, with hardly any light coming through the trees.

'Oh!' said Freya. 'I've no idea where we are, but we can't have walked far.'

Megan reached for Freya's hand. She began to feel worried.

'I think we've walked further than we meant to,' she said. 'We need to go home. Everyone's going to be worried.'

'I think it's this way,' said Freya, suddenly feeling

a bit braver. 'I'm sure this is right.'

They walked for a few steps, still holding hands. But it didn't feel right.

'This isn't right,' said Freya.

'Oh no,' said Megan and she felt her eyes fill with tears. She wasn't only worried about being lost, she was worried about her mum and dad worrying.

Now it was Freya's turn to reassure Megan.

'It's OK, Meggy,' she said. 'We'll find a way out soon. Let's try this way.'

So they turned and walked the other way. But they were still surrounded by trees. Soon they didn't even know which direction they were facing and which way they had come.

They tried another direction, still holding hands tightly. But that didn't feel right either!

'Oh, Freya, we're completely lost,' said Megan, feeling the tears start to fall. 'What are we going to do?'

Megan felt more afraid than she could ever

remember, and at that exact moment, something very unexpected happened.

Suddenly, Freya stopped walking. 'Megan,' she said. 'Look.'

Standing a few metres away from them, his fur shining brightly, was a beautiful big, golden dog. Buttercup!

Buttercup
to the Rescue

The girls stood silently as the golden dog walked slowly towards them. Megan and Freya looked at each other in amazement. Soon Buttercup was standing right in front of them.

'Buttercup,' said Freya. 'Is it really you?'

But she knew it was, and Megan knew too. Buttercup looked straight at Megan then.

'He's going to help us,' said Megan, turning to Freya. 'He's going to help us get home. Oh, I'm so glad you're here,' she said to Buttercup, suddenly feeling a whole lot better. 'I thought we were lost forever.'

Buttercup looked steadily at Megan for a moment, and Megan understood what he was thinking, just as she'd understood Dorothy.

'That's what they're here for,' Megan said.

'What do you mean?' said Freya.

'Buttercup, Dorothy and the mice,' said Megan, a big smile lighting up her face. 'They're here to protect us.'

'To protect us?' said Freya. 'Like when they helped Granny and Jonathon?'

'Exactly!' said Megan, nodding. And Buttercup seemed to nod too.

Buttercup turned around then, and stood between the two girls. Freya looked puzzled.

'He wants to lead us out,' said Megan. 'He wants us to hold on to his coat.'

So the girls held on to Buttercup's soft coat as he

started to walk back through the wood. They didn't know where they were going, but they just knew that Buttercup was leading them to safety.

Before long, they were out in the open again. The sky was really dark and it was threatening to rain again, but Buttercup stopped and looked straight at Freya.

'I think he wants us to wait here,' said Freya.

The girls smiled at each other. Somehow, they both seemed to be able to understand him. Buttercup walked away from them, sniffing the ground. Then, he turned and walked back towards them. Hanging from his mouth was Freya's missing friendship bracelet.

'My bracelet!' gasped Freya. 'Oh, thank you.'

Freya took the bracelet from Buttercup's soft mouth and gave him an enormous hug. Then the girls walked on either side of Buttercup as he led them back through the field, and as they walked, they stroked his soft, warm head.

It wasn't long before the small bridge was in sight. Then Buttercup stopped, looking up at Megan.

'I think he needs to leave now,' Megan said to Freya.

'Will we see you again?' Freya asked, reaching out to stroke him.

Buttercup turned to Freya and nuzzled his nose in the palm of her hand.

'I hope we do,' said Megan.

'Me too,' said Freya.

Then Buttercup turned and moved towards the wood. Just at that moment, they felt the first drop of rain. The girls watched as Buttercup sped up, his golden coat blowing in the breeze. He stopped at the edge of the wood and turned to look at them, then disappeared into the trees.

'Come on, let's go,' said Freya. 'Before we get soaked.'

She grabbed hold of Megan's hand and they raced

across the little bridge. Just as they reached the other side, they saw Freya's mum come out of the house. She waved to them as they ran up the garden.

'I was looking for you,' she called. 'Where on earth did you get to?'

'We went to look for this,' said Freya, holding up her wrist with her friendship bracelet on.

'Come on, quick,' said Freya's mum, grabbing the girls' hands and running with them back into the house as the rain came down in big drops.

'Do you want a flapjack?' she asked them, as they stepped into the kitchen and out of the rain. 'They've just come out of the oven.'

'Ooh, yes please,' said Freya. 'I bet these are even yummier than Granny's shortbread.'

Later, when Megan was tucked up in bed, she thought about what an amazing few days she'd had. Here she was, living in a big house *and* there was a big fluffy dog too, just like in the game she used to play in her head. She could hardly believe the exciting things that had happened since she had moved to Buttercup House. And today, seeing Buttercup and him helping them, had been wonderful.

Megan thought about how Buttercup had looked at her and how she had known then that the animals were protecting them. Suddenly, she realised something. Each of the animals was good at something. The mice helped children remember, Dorothy stopped them from feeling lonely and warned them about hidden dangers, and Buttercup was good at finding things. After all, he'd found Freya's bracelet and helped them find their way out of the wood. Then she realised something else that Buttercup was good at. He was good at being kind and understanding. Megan felt as if she could ask his help for anything and that he wouldn't mind at all.

As she drifted off to sleep, Megan thought about the animals. *Our very own protectors,* she thought.

A
Rainbow Treehouse

That night, it poured with rain. All day Sunday, Megan looked out for Dorothy, but there was no sign of her. *I bet she's tucked up warm and dry,* thought Megan. Then she thought about Buttercup and hoped he was nice and dry under the trees. She wondered if she should make him a coat, and imagined what colour it would be and how lovely he would look in it. She could just picture him in a big black and white checked blanket coat, all soft and snugly and tied with a black ribbon.

On Monday, it rained all the way to school, and then it carried on raining. The headmaster put a *Wet Play* sign on the main door, which meant no playing outside at lunch.

'What are we going to do?' Megan asked Freya.

'We could go to Lego club,' Freya suggested.

Megan didn't really want to, but what else were they going to do?

'We could make a Lego treehouse,' Freya said.

'A yellow one, with red stripes,' agreed Megan.

'And a blue ladder,' added Freya.

Perhaps it would be fun after all.

The girls found a space on the rug in Year One's classroom and spread the bricks out in front of them until they had enough to make the walls.

'I bet this one won't be six steps by five,' said Megan.

'It won't even be one step by one, will it?' laughed Freya.

Alex and Thomas, from their form, came over and asked the girls what they were doing.

'We're making a treehouse,' said Freya.

'Can we help?' said Alex. He loved treehouses.

The girls both nodded.

'Megan has a treehouse in her garden that we play in,' said Freya. 'This one's going to be yellow and red and blue.'

'Wow!' Alex said to Megan. 'You're so lucky. I'd love a treehouse! Do you play there a lot?'

'All the time,' said Megan. 'It's mine and Freya's special place and we have books in there and pens and things.'

'You're so lucky,' Alex said. 'It's so busy at my house, with my baby brother and two sisters, that I can never have anyone over.'

'You'll have to pretend that this is your treehouse, Alex,' said Freya, 'and these little people are us.'

The children all laughed. They had a great time building the treehouse and called it their rainbow house.

'It's a treehouse of many colours,' said Megan. 'Just like a rainbow.'

In bed that night, Megan thought about Alex and his very busy house and she wondered if Freya was thinking about him too. *He's so friendly,* thought Megan. *It'd be so nice if he could have friends round.* And as she closed her eyes, she found herself thinking about Buttercup and how kind he was, and somehow, it comforted her. She thought about how he had helped Granny and Jonathon, and how he had helped her and Freya too. And she remembered how she had felt that the animals were protecting them.

Megan crossed her fingers and hoped that maybe, just maybe, Buttercup would be able to help Alex too.

If you like *Buttercup Magic*, you'll love:

Ruth Symes

Bella Donna

Illustrated
by Marion
Lindsay

Most girls dream of being a princess, but Bella
Donna has always longed to be a witch. The only
thing she wants more is to find a family to take her
out of the children's home where she lives. But no
one seems quite right, until she meets Lilith.

With Lilith's help, will Bella Donna be able to
make both of her secret wishes come true?

www.BellaDonnaOnline.co.uk